DOM X

SOUL SISTERS

HER WHIP WAS
harder
THAN HER
late

SOUL SISTERS

DOM X

Cover and Title Art: © Pretty in Ink 2023

Editor: Messenger's Memos

Formatter: © DAZED Designs 2023

"I refuse to live in the ordinary world as ordinary women, to enter ordinary relationships. I want ecstasy."

— UNKNOWN

A NOTE TO THE READERS

Please be aware that this story is based in the UK and therefore is written with British spelling in mind.

Dom X is an MF short story focusing on a Dom/Sub relationship. It does contain strictly adult content and is recommended for readers over the age of 18.

Enjoy.

BLURB

As a sought-after personal assistant and a private Dominatrix, Neala has spent the last ten years living a double life.

No longer content with just any sub and not getting any younger, she longs to find the right guy to share in her alternate lifestyle and to settle down with.

A routine night out at Dom X reveals a surprising twist.

Has Neala finally found everything she's been looking for?

Julian Taylor has always been pushed to do better and be better, and no one pushes him more than himself. However, this lifestyle he leads is not who he really is.

Hiding his true self and desires from the people in his life has never been more difficult.

After meeting his new personal assistant, Neala, Julian finds himself needing an outlet.

Taking a trip to Dom X, a nightclub for the not so faint-hearted, Julian finds just what he's looking for. A brunette beauty who has a way of handling him, and a whip.

But those liquid honey eyes behind the mask are all too familiar to him . . .

NEALA

I do not want to deal with another snivelling, chauvinistic rich boy right now. I'm so freaking sick of the power-hungry dickwads that come through this door. While this company might be impressive as hell, the bosses I've had the misfortune of working for have been anything but.

The majority of the time, the guys that come in here seem to think it's acceptable to grab my ass like a piece of meat and stare at my titties like they hold the answers to the universe, and I'm so over it. If I have to deal with one more of them, I'm going to pull my whip out and show them how powerful I really am.

Looking up at the clock, I scowl at the time. My new boss, Mr Julian Taylor, is already five minutes late. Excellent. What a great first impression. I roll my eyes and continue typing up the weekly report, deciding that just because they don't know how to do their job, doesn't give me licence to slack off at mine.

I get completely immersed in the work before me and don't realise there's someone in front of me until a man with a deep voice clears his throat. Without looking up and continuing to type, I pass over a stack of papers and say automatically, "Good morning, sir. Welcome to Odyssey Corp. If you need any assistance, just press one on the phone. There is a map of the building and emergency exits in your paperwork, as well as an update on all the current cases."

When the man before me remains where he is without any sign of moving, I look up at him and suck in a sharp breath at how ridiculously gorgeous he is. I was not prepared for that. I'd love to see this guy on his knees before me, begging for me to let him cum.

Mr Taylor's dark eyes and hair both surprise and arouse me. I knew he was Scottish, but I certainly wasn't expecting tall, dark, and handsome. I assumed wrongly that he'd be a middle-aged redhead, with a sour expression and a dismissive attitude. The man before me is anything but. His warm skin tone, twinkling eyes, and pleasant smile shock me almost as much as his young age. There's no way this guy is more than two years older than me.

"It's a pleasure to meet you, Miss . . . ?" Mr Taylor rolls his 'r' in a way that has my knees rubbing together under the desk. *If it's pleasure he's asking for, I'll be happy to provide it. If he behaves.*

Snapping myself out of my dirty thoughts, I focus on

his words and answer, "My apologies, Mr Taylor. I'm Neala McCourt, but you can call me Neala."

I rise from the chair and reach my hand out for him to shake, my eyes meeting his. While he may be my boss, the Dom inside me refuses to back down from strong eye contact. The desire to control the situation is always unyielding.

Leaning slightly over my office desk, his hand meets mine, and I'm pleased to find that Mr Taylor lets me dominate the grip between us. *Good boy*.

He clears his throat and steps back with a small nod. "Neala," he replies in an almost whisper. "That's a lovely name. Very unique. By all means, please call me Julian. Mr Taylor sounds like my father."

"When there are no clients here I will, but otherwise, I'll stick to the formality, if you don't mind."

As he's my boss, it's only right that I keep it as formal as I can, especially when he's looking like *that*. I need to remember that, in this place, Julian is above me. If I lower my guard, my wayward thoughts of bending him over my desk and spanking him might accidentally slip through, and I can't have that.

Not wanting to be around the temptation, I abruptly say, "If there's nothing else, I have a lot of paperwork I need to get sorted this morning," and sit back down in my seat.

Julian's eyes seem hooded, and he nods immediately. "That's all, thank you," he replies, almost running into his office and closing the door behind him.

Well, this should be interesting, I think to myself,

enjoying watching his tight ass as he retreats. I do love the way he says thank you.

JULIAN

Almost running into my office like some scatterbrained teenager who can't handle his hormones, I close the door and inhale a deep breath. Steadying myself, I square my shoulders and walk around the solid black desk in the middle of the huge office. Pulling out the chair, I take a seat. I give myself a moment to gather my thoughts, trying to clear out the brunette beauty currently flooding my mind, and making me nearly flood my boxers too.

Never have I been floored by such a firecracker. The moment Neala locked eyes with me and didn't once even shift her gaze a fraction, my existence went to shit. I'm normally met with nervous glances and stuttered words. I may be high-end and rich, but that doesn't mean I don't hold secrets about what I truly want in a woman. Neala, however, rocked me to my core with a single look. I can only imagine what she could do to me if I was bound and on my knees for her.

Physically shaking myself out of those images as my cock twitches against my tailored black trousers, I try to focus on what I'm actually meant to be doing, before my fantasising sends me back out of this office to see how far I can push my stunning new PA. See what it takes to get those delectable hands spanking my ass—

I grasp the stack of papers Neala handed me and begin to flip through them, looking but not absorbing what words are written on each piece. It's no use, though. Neala planted a seed when her liquid honey eyes ensnared me, and I'm sitting here watering it with each dirty thought of her demanding my obedience.

Well, fuck. A cold shower is what I need. Settling for the next best thing, I pour myself a glass of cold water from the pitcher on the desk, focusing on the chilled liquid tracking its way down my throat. After finishing the glass, I finally feel a little more focused on the task at hand and begin flipping through the papers again, this time taking in a little more information than the previous attempt.

After analysing each page and calming myself enough to realise what I'm here to be doing, I get up and take in my new surroundings. The open office has a perfectly simple black-and-white décor, and there's not a speck out of place. Obviously, someone with a flair for making 'simple' look beautiful dressed this office, from the tall black cabinets situated on the left side, to the crisp-white tiled floor. Yet, the quirky abstract mirror on one wall compliments the structured triangle artwork on the opposite wall. I make my way over to the floor-to-ceiling window, which spans the entire length of the office as well. Reaching out, I pull the beaded string and the slatted blinds begin to recoil, revealing the view of the city stretched out before me.

Something about cities always sends a rush through

my veins. The hustle and bustle of people coming and going all hours of the day, the cars lining the streets, and at night the amazing displays of lights that bring the place to life even more than the daylight does.

A knock on the door jolts me from my musing, and I snap back to reality.

"Please, come in." As the words leave my mouth, there's only one thought zooming around my mind: Neala, and how I could bend her over the desk, or better yet, how she could bend *me* over the desk.

"Good afternoon, Mr Taylor," Neala formally addresses me as her stilettos click on the floor. Each purposefully placed stride demands attention as she makes her way to the desk, files in hand.

I can't help—or stop—my eyes momentarily flicking to her luscious long legs as she walks, tanned to perfection and so sleek her skin reflects the fluorescent light.

"Eyes up here, Julian." At Neala's demand, my eyes immediately snap back to hers. "Good," she praises, and I swallow hard.

Clenching my jaw, I unexpectedly drop my gaze from her overpowering stare. I don't miss the twitch of a smile at the corner of her delicious mouth.

This woman, or seductress, should I say, is going to ruin me, and I find myself far too excited by the prospect of it.

2

NEALA

Focus, I remind myself, trying to ignore the way Julian's easy submission makes my core slick with need.

Clearly, it's been too long since I've let my Dom side out, if the way I'm responding to my new boss is anything to go by. I'm lucky he didn't respond badly to me chastising him over the eye fucking he was giving my legs.

Without a moment's hesitation, I decide that I'll be going to Dom X tonight. If I'm lucky, I might even find a tall, dark, and handsome sub to take my most recent desires out on. My lip twitches in anticipation, and I turn my attention back to Julian.

"I wanted to see if you'd like me to order you something specific for lunch, and if you have any allergies or intolerances I should know about for future reference." I could have easily asked him over the intercom, but frankly, I just needed to see if he was still as hot as I pictured, and—fuck me—he's even better.

Julian waves his hand at me dismissively and mumbles, "Don't worry about it," before picking up his phone and turning away to face the window.

Oh no, you did not.

I stand my ground, my eyes narrowing into angry slits as I say between clenched teeth, "I insist."

Julian continues to type mindlessly on his phone in silence, while I awkwardly wait for an appropriate answer, my anger at being dismissed rising. After a few minutes, I clear my throat loudly to garner his attention, and his head pops up, turning toward me with confusion written all over his face.

"Sorry. Did you need something?" He seems surprised that I'm still standing in his office.

Now livid, I ask one more time, "Lunch?"

"What about it?" His flippant response has my patience snapping.

"Right. Here's the deal, Mr Taylor. I may have a position lower than you in this company, but at no time will I accept anything other than respect. When I ask you a question, I expect a prompt, polite answer, and at no point is anything less appropriate. If we plan on having a productive and effective working relationship, I suggest you listen well, *sir*. Without me to do all of your dirty work, you will find this job becoming rapidly overwhelming," I rant while he gawks at me. "Now, what would you like for lunch, Mr Taylor?"

Silence greets me for a moment before he answers

nervously, "Sandwich?"

I nod, smiling in approval. "Anything in particular?" He shakes his head. "Good. Allergies or intolerances?"

"No. I like pretty much all food, except apples," Julian answers promptly.

I lick my lips, pleased with his quick change in behaviour. With deliberate steps, I approach him until we are mere inches apart and then straighten his mauve tie, my gaze drinking up all his attention. I pat his shoulders, wiping away non-existent lint. Julian swallows hard, his Adam's apple bobbing, and it gives away how nervous he is to have my hands on him. "I think we'll get along just fine."

With that, I turn and leave, unable to keep the extra sway out of my hips as I do, feeling the burn of his heavy gaze on my ass until the door closes behind me. I exhale a breath and sit behind my desk, relieved that I got out of there before I got myself fired.

Picking up the phone, I dial the café downstairs and order a mix of sandwiches for the both of us, and as I hang up, I catch Julian looking at me through the glass beside his door. He quickly disappears, and I smile smugly as I get back to work, delighted that I'm getting under his skin too.

JULIAN

I head back to my desk, my heart still doing a rapid tap dance against my ribs. The proximity of Neala and her sweet jasmine scent, which engulfed my senses when she brushed my shoulders, is still riding me hard. I don't know how I didn't grab that sexy ass of hers, wrap her legs around my waist, and take her on the desk. I've a feeling if I had, though, it might have been me who would have been in trouble. I seriously need to get my itch scratched.

Sliding my thumb across my phone, I reopen the Google app. The Dom X website pops back up. I had been so distracted trying to find somewhere to go later, I hadn't even realised Neala was still standing in the office with me. The way she put me in my place when I tried to brush her off had me scared and horny at the same time.

Highlighting the address for the club, I find it on my maps and see it's not too far away. I breathe a sigh of relief that hopefully after tonight I'll be feeling a little less sexually frustrated. Tomorrow, I'll be able to concentrate on the work I'm here to do, and not focus on how good Neala's pussy would feel wrapped around my dick if I fuck her on the desk.

Thinking of the Devil, however, in struts Neala, a tray of sandwiches balanced in one hand. I jump up to take the tray from her and place them on the desk.

"Thank you, Mr Taylor." The way my name rolls off her tongue has my balls tightening. That voice and demanding essence would have me doing anything this seductress asked of me.

I watch in raw, male ecstasy as Neala picks up a sandwich and wraps her lips around it, biting down, then chewing and swallowing. Her tongue darts out and runs over her luscious, plump upper lip. I all but moan at the move. Not realising what I'm doing, I suddenly take a step forward into Neala's space, knowing I shouldn't have the moment her golden eyes flare like fire.

Neala holds my gaze with a heated stare, and my Adam's apple bobs. Not this time. I won't back down this time. I'm a good eight inches taller than her, so I push further into her space until her chin tips to keep her eyes locked on mine.

Moments, maybe even minutes, pass between us. Neither of us utters a word, just a continuous battle for dominance wars between our eyes. My blood turns to fire in my veins as it heads south without a single touch.

I won't back down. I won't back down. The mantra playing over and over in my mind is losing, however. All I want to do is drop to my knees and beg for punishment.

Neala's red-stained lips part on a shuddered breath, an indication I'm having just as much effect on her as she's having on me.

My lips part. "Neala . . ."

The office phone rings so loud we both jump, and the chemistry that was brewing and bubbling is shattered.

Neala marches out of the office so hard I'm surprised her stilettos don't snap.

I fall like a felled tree into the chair and catch myself on the desk before I wheel across the office from the force.

Releasing a huge breath, I bury my head in my hands. What the actual fuck just happened? More to the point, why?

I definitely need a night at Dom X.

3

NEALA

Sucking in, I pull one last time on my leather corset strings before tying them off, the thrill of anticipation thrumming through my veins. *I'm so ready for tonight.*

With no small level of pride, I take in my image mirrored back to me through the full-length reflective glass. I've never lacked in self-love. While my body is far from perfect, it's mine and I love every curve on it, and more than that, I love how it can bring a grown man to his knees.

I stifle a groan at the sudden mental visual of bringing Julian to his. Knowing that it's never going to happen, I shake my head to clear my thoughts, my dark, loose curls falling over my bare shoulders.

Bending over awkwardly, I start pulling on my first thigh-high stiletto boot, slipping my foot in easily before slowly drawing up the small zip. I let my fingers softly caress the length of my leg as I go, enjoying the build in anticipation it brings. I pull on the other boot in the same fashion and stand tall, taking one last look at my almost complete leather ensemble. The outfit complements wickedly with my thickly lined black cat eyes, flushed cheeks, and deep-red lips.

Stalking to the armchair with all the confidence I feel thrumming through my veins, I pluck up my soft black trench coat, gliding my arms through the holes and tying it securely at my waist. No one would know how much—or, more specifically, how little—I have on underneath, and that idea alone makes my core clench.

Picking up my bag with my signature dominatrix mask hidden inside, I leave my apartment and head out to my longed-for destination: Dom X.

* * *

The heady beat of sensual music blasts through the lush red entryway of Dom X. I secure my mask while the doorman takes my bag and coat, careful to keep his eyes downcast from mine like a good boy.

"Is there anything I can help you with tonight, Mistress?" the large man asks in a respectful tone, and I smirk, loving being in my element.

"Not tonight, pet. I'm after something specific tonight, and I'm afraid you aren't quite what I'm looking for," I reply, taking in his overly bulky body and dirty blond hair. *No, no. Only tall, dark, and handsome for me this evening.*

14

I step in through the heavy ruby drapery and let the steady beat lick over my skin, the volume and bass increasing with every step of my seven-inch heels.

The hall feeds into a large, open area with various subs dancing and writhing on poles, in cages, and on stages around the room. I look around with interest, not wanting to waste my time socialising tonight as my pussy pulses with my need for control.

I take in the people around me while making a beeline for the bar. To my disappointment, none of the men available come even slightly close to the image I desire for tonight.

"Dirty Martini, Mistress?" the bartender asks me, and I'm always pleased with her memory. After all, Dom X is my addiction of choice, and I'm definitely a regular.

With a flourish of my hand in affirmation, she runs off to do my bidding, and I sigh as I turn toward her, watching her make it just the way I like it. *At least I'll get a good drink out of tonight if all else fails.*

Someone brushes gently against my shoulder, and I turn with a frown to find my long-time friend, Jasmine, smiling at me, with her sub leashed and on his knees at her feet.

"Hey, Chicky, why so blue?" she asks me, and I smile in response, always happy to see her.

I pick up my drink as it gets delivered to me and shake my head at her, taking a sip before I answer, enjoying the delicious burn. "Alas, there's not a good choice in sight. Maybe I should settle down like you have. It seems to give you a never-ending smile." I'm only half-joking because I've never seen my friend happier since she found her pet.

"All jokes aside, you should," she answers, playing with his hair mindlessly. "And what are you talking about? There's prime meat all through this room. Look at that guy. He's practically begging for a spanking."

I take another sip and look over at the short ginger-haired man in his sub mask and red leather pants, and I scrunch up my nose in disinterest. "Nope. I'm feeling particular tonight. My new boss has gotten me on edge, and I need to take it out on someone."

"You? Wanting to dominate an old guy? Since when?" Jasmine asks, the shock evident on her face, and I can't help but laugh.

"No. Yuck." I laugh harder. "He's fucking hot as hell, if I'm being honest, and his ass is delicious. Good enough to bite or fuck, and to my horror, I spent the whole day envisioning doing just that." I shake my head at how annoying it is having him dominate my mind all day when the only one of us that should be *dominating* is me.

She takes a sip of her drink and nods in understanding. "It's a shame he's your boss. There's not much you can do about that. Alright, what's he look like? I'll help you find an outlet because you look like you need it, bad!"

I groan quiet enough that only she can hear me. "Smooth caramel skin, short dark hair, hot as fuck, and tall enough to make me want to tower over him."

"Well, looks like your luck just picked up because that yummy recipe just walked in."

My back straightens, and I follow her gaze to the entrance, where a very nervous-looking specimen glances around the room. He's wearing tiny black leather shorts, revealing a bulge that's anything but small, a black and teal corset that shows off strong pecs, and arms that make me drool just a little, and I'm not talking about my mouth.

"Fuck yes," I growl, jumping off the seat before I slip off. "Don't wait up," I joke, stalking toward my prey, leaving my friend laughing in my wake.

The tall, dark, and handsome catches my gaze as I approach before dropping his submissively, his body facing mine in acknowledgement. "Are you looking for a play partner tonight?" I'm direct, wanting to get straight to the point.

Sometimes I like to socialise a bit more, but I'm in the zone and don't want to waste my time with somebody who's taken or not interested in my gender. At least it's simple to define who is dominant and who isn't by the mask requirement of Dom X. It keeps things simple for even the newest members.

"Yes, Ma'am. I am," he tells me simply, his mask a plain black one, not an embellishment in sight.

"Call me Mistress," I say, feeling hopeful. "I'm looking for full company tonight, and if you're interested, you can join me as my sub while we're here. What do you say?"

While I may be the dominant, it's important to always have consent and understanding between us, in order to have a safe and fulfilling night for both of us.

"I'd like that, Mistress. I'm looking for the same thing," he tells me.

I smile, eager to get started because he's perfect. "Excellent. Just so you're aware, I don't share."

He nods agreeably and kneels before me, with his head low and his arms upturned. *Oh, he is a good boy.* "Follow me, and we can go to one of the back rooms to get better acquainted—and you can tell me your safeword."

I hope he likes pegging.

4

JULIAN

Safeword, oh, this Mistress is everything I need. Standing, I follow the beauty to a back room, every nerve in my body tingling in anticipation with each step I take.

We enter the room, and Mistress clicks the door locked behind us. As she does, I knowingly kneel again with my palms turned up and my head bowed.

"Safeword? Also, any limits you have," Mistress requests.

"Pilgrim, Mistress, and no limits, just the safeword," I reply, not that I'll be using it. I need whatever she's going to dole out to me.

The vision of Neala pinning me to the desk has been plaguing me over and over all afternoon. I hear the zipper of a bag opening behind me, and I shudder as the cool of a leather whip strokes across the nape of my neck.

"Undress." The single command has me untying my

corset hurriedly, then pulling my tight shorts down to my feet in a swift movement. "Leave your thong on," the Mistress' slightly breathy voice adds as my fingers grip the sides. The black thong was a last-minute choice, and by her reaction, I'm glad I put it on.

As per Dom X rules, I keep my mask in place. The deep navy is almost black, and it covers three-quarters of my face, from my forehead to just above my lips. I kneel once again, my cock already twitching in excitement.

The leather of the whip smooths its way down my spine. Every inch it slowly slinks down sends roaring fire through my veins. As it reaches the top of one of my ass cheeks, Mistress flicks her wrist, and the sting is everything I've been waiting for all day. I can't hold in the whimpered moan that escapes my mouth.

"Lean forward."

I heed her demand instantly, and I'm rewarded with a strike across both cheeks. Delicious euphoria blasts through my body and settles in my cock. Sting after sting bites my ass and pre-cum dampens my thong.

"Oh, you are a good boy." Mistress stops, coming to stand in front of me, and lifts my chin with the whip.

For a fleeting moment, I make eye contact, and I'm sure those honey eyes belong to Neala. Giving myself a mental shake, I tell myself to snap out of seeing her everywhere I look. Just because I'd give anything for Neala to be the one, she isn't.

Mistress begins to undress, punctuating each word as she does. "Now, before I have my fun with you, I'll have something first."

Containing my somewhat adolescent excitement, I continue to kneel, waiting in anticipation for my next command. Mistress, now completely naked, lowers herself to the plush rug before me and spreads her legs. I almost growl inhumanly at her slick, bald pussy. I swallow hard, my mouth watering in anticipation of tasting her. I watch, ensnared, as Mistress runs her fingers between her glistening pussy lips and then raises her hand to her mouth, snaking her tongue out to lick them clean. Her moan has me almost moving, but I remain where I am. I do not move until told.

"Come find out how good I taste."

I'm moving without thinking, hooking my arms under her sleek legs and lapping like I've found an oasis in the desert. She tastes like pure heaven. Each pass of my tongue over her clit has her legs shaking in my hold. I gorge myself on her, a glutton for more. Moving lower, I spear my tongue as deep into her as I can. The desired noise of pure pleasure fills the room, and it's music to my ears, spurring me on to fuck her with my tongue till she squirts all over my face.

Mistress' breathing and whining become faster and shorter as I push her closer and closer. Her release hits so fast and hard I'm almost not ready, but I drink her down, riding out her orgasm. Through her whimpered moans, I'm sure I hear her say Julian, but I brush it off as hope on my part.

I remove myself from between her exquisite legs and go back to kneeling, leaving her release on my face, not wanting to lose it just yet. My cock is throbbing painfully, and I ache to grasp it and pump at least once, but I remain still. To my absolute shock and delight, Mistress turns around on her hands and knees, spreads her legs, and presents her dripping pussy and sexy little asshole to me. Slightly stumped, I don't move.

"You had better fuck better than you eat pussy."

I pull my cock from my thong, slide on a condom from beside me, then I surge forward. I plough into her so fast, even I'm taken by surprise. Her walls grip my dick like a vice, and it takes everything not to cum right then and there. I squeeze my eyes closed and grind my teeth, regaining myself before I do.

5

NEALA

The sub's cock stretches me more than I'd expected, considering how much he just made me cum. His girth fills me to perfection, his length hitting nerves deep inside, and the amazing feeling slips from my mouth as pure pleasure.

I've never let a sub take me from behind before, and I didn't even realise I was turning around for him until I told him he better fuck me better than he ate me.

As his hips begin to roll, and his cock rocks in and out of my pussy, I soon find out he definitely can fuck better than he eats—and take it from me, that's one hell of a feat to achieve. He's also good at teasing me. His movements are just slow enough to push me to the cliff's edge, but never hard or quick enough to shove me off it.

Remembering who's the Dom here—eventually—I

order him, "Fuck me harder and faster." If I had eyes in the back of my head, I'm pretty sure he'd be smirking with smugness because that order came out more as a whined plea.

Being a good boy, though, the sub obliges my plea—no, order! Three harder pumps of his hips, and I cum hard enough to bite back a curse.

A slightly embarrassing, breathy mess, I try to regain myself and what I'm meant to be. I haven't been fucked so good in a long, long time. It's normally me doing the fucking, and that's what I need my addled brain to remember right now. I get to my shaking legs, hiding that fact as best I can, and turn back to the sub. He's back in his kneeling position; he's certainly a well-practised one. I take a good eyeful of his large, solid cock poking out of his sexy thong, still condom-covered and standing at attention. He can also last like a pro too.

Opening my bag again, I grip the smooth leather handle of my flogger. "Take that off and get on all fours." I push as much authority into my words as I can. The sub carefully removes and ties off the sheath, tucking it neatly out of the way before placing his palms on the floor and pushing his peachy ass into the air. Damn, he's good.

I make my way around him, taking in every bronzed and honed inch of his body. I pause as I see a birthmark on the crest of his right hip, thinking how hot it looks; weird, I know, but we all like what we like, right?

Before I can let myself get caught up in the sub too much, I bring the leather tassels of the flogger down on his sweet cheeks. He doesn't even tense. I do it again, harder this time. Nothing. This sub is revving me up. I might end up with him in me again, instead of the other way around. I bring the flogger across his now pink and marked cheeks. This time I get a reaction. The sub whines in pleasure, and I watch as more pre-cum drips from his cock.

I can't take it anymore. I head back to my bag of fun and pull out the sleek black strap-on and bottle of lube. Securing the harness around me, I make my way back to the sexy ass I've been eager to have since coming in here. The image of this being Julian pushes me on further. A girl can dream.

The sub's words from earlier about having no real limits, just his safeword if I go too far, send a shiver through me again.

"I hope you're ready." Not a question, just a statement, because if he isn't ready and willing, he knows what to say.

The sub doesn't reply, just waits patiently like a good boy. For his good behaviour, I give his right ass cheek a spank and smile at the little moan that escapes his lips. I squirt the bottle of lube into my hand and rub it up and down the strap-on, then I get to work on his ass. When he's slick enough, I push my middle finger into him. In and out, in and out, getting his ass ready and the sub more worked up. As he begins pushing back on me, I insert another finger, stretching him further. The whine I'm rewarded with is perfect.

Getting to my knees behind him, I remove my fingers and slowly tease him with the silicon cock, dipping just the tip in and out. Then I go deeper and deeper, till the strap-on is to the hilt. From the vibrations I feel in his body as I grip his hips, he's absolutely loving it. I begin to draw back, then slide back into him, a little harder this time. As I pick up my rhythm and rotation of my hips, his moans become faster. I plunge back in harder and give his sweet ass another spank as I do.

"Look at you taking it so well," I coo.

Placing my palm in the middle of his back, I push until his chest is flush with the floor. This way there's no give as I begin to drive harder in and out of him. Fuck, this is just what I needed. Seeing this well-built and sexy man on his front for me as I plough deeper and harder into him has me needing to cum again.

"You ready to cum for me?"

"Yes, Mistress." He sounds like he's holding back his orgasm so hard.

Taking one last full thrust from me, my obedient sub lets out that deep whine of male ecstasy and cums perfectly.

Breathing hard and with slightly burning thighs, I pull free from him as he lays like a panting mess on his front, trying to recover.

I pack all my belongings away and redress. I'm done for the night, and now that I've had my fun, I want to go home. As I turn back around, the sub is also finishing dressing. He drops his eyes to the floor.

"Same time next week?" I ask, a little lost for words. I shock myself at that question; not many subs I've asked to meet a second time. There's just something about this one.

"Yes, Mistress."

With that answer, I'm unlocking the door and exiting the room before I end up undressing him again and riding that exquisite cock.

6

JULIAN

I make my way back to my apartment, feeling fully satisfied with how the night went. The Mistress was everything I needed, and I'll need it again after a week of working with Neala. Goddammit, she knew what she was doing, yet I'm still shocked at her bending over and letting me take her. Each thrust I imagined it being Neala's tight pussy squeezing my cock, and how the fuck I didn't cum, I don't know. I fall fast asleep when my head hits the pillow and don't move till my alarm the next morning.

I'm surprised as I enter my office that Neala hasn't arrived yet, but I continue with the paperwork I should have looked at yesterday. At least today, I'm more focused on what I've got to do.

The door swings open and Neala bustles through, a coffee cup in each hand, and a smile spread across her stunning face. Just like that, I can't remember what I'm meant to be doing. The mouth-watering aroma of earthy coffee mixed with a sweet hint of caramel hits me, and some sense of stability washes back over me.

"Got you a coffee. Sorry I'm late. The queue was longer than I expected." Neala hands the takeaway cup to me, and I take a tentative sip.

Releasing a moan of contentment, the rustic yet sweet liquid tracks down my throat and blankets my soul.

"Thank you. What's on the agenda today?" Noticing the pep in her step as she turns and shuts the door, I also don't miss how the abrasive assertiveness has dimmed a little—for now, at least.

I find myself enjoying this side of Neala, not that I don't like her 'no shit taking' other side too. She moves around the office, gathering files as she goes, like a well-oiled machine—so at ease in an environment some might find daunting. My eyes drift from her white blouse to her sexy ass in the tight grey pencil skirt, black stilettos accentuating her luscious legs. My mind delves into last night, and my cock suddenly stands at attention.

Think about tables.

Think about nothing.

Think about driving deep into . . . no, no, no.

"Julian?" The snap in Neala's voice tells me this isn't the first time she's tried to gain my attention.

"Sorry, yes? Sorry, I was in a world of my own." I stutter my way back to reality.

"This file is the next case, but there are parts missing. I need to find them, but while I do, you need to go through it." She places the file on my desk, and I'm thankful the conversation is like ice water over my libido.

* * *

Over the next few days, we learn to work in sync with one another, and I become more than just a horny teenager around Neala. The working relationship we are building is better than I've ever had with anyone, and my respect for her grows with each day.

Come Thursday morning, I find myself excited to head to the office, but also a little apprehensive about what I'm doing tomorrow evening at Dom X. I've never felt torn before about wanting what I want, and wanting a woman I work with. I feel like I'm betraying her. That thought pulls me up short. Giving myself a mental shake, I finish fastening my tie and make my way to work.

I'm just about to hang my blazer on the hook on my office door when it opens, and I clash against Neala as she comes through, coffee in hand. The burning liquid ends up all over me and a very stunned-looking Neala who starts spouting profanities and something about it being my fault that I'm behind the door. All I can think about is getting the fucking shirt off me. I remove it so fast, I pop the buttons clean off.

Once off, I use the dry part to wipe myself down. Satisfied that the fires of hell are no longer burning me, I look up, straight into the seductive honey eyes of Neala. Those eyes then drop to the birthmark that crests my hip. She glances back up, and what I can only describe as a look of knowing crosses her face before an expression of deep satisfaction settles on it.

"Sub?"

The one word leaves her plush lips on a whisper, but it's all I need.

"Mistress."

We clash once again as her hands grip my hair, and my mouth covers hers. I reach out to push the door shut as she liquefies against me, and I grab her thighs, lifting her. The skirt rolls up as I wrap her legs around me, and I make my way to the desk.

Pulling her mouth free from my bruising kiss, she says breathlessly, "This isn't the way it should be, sub."

A wicked grin spreads across my face as I sit her down on my desk, and Neala's look eggs me on. "You're in my office now, Neala." Her eyes widen on her name. "You do as you're told in here." I consume her mouth again.

Forcing her skirt higher, my fingers connect with her slick pussy lips—no panties in my way, *thank fuck*. I lock my other hand around her throat and guide her to lie back. She whines beneath me, and I feel her swallow, the movement sending a spike of heat through me.

"You'll be swallowing my cock soon." I plunge two fingers into her tightness, capturing her moan with my mouth as I lean down and kiss her again.

Working her over and over until she is writhing and panting, I feel her tighten, and I curl my fingers, stroking that sweet spot through her release as she squirts onto my hand.

"Good girl." I let go of her throat and allow her to sit up. "Now, on your knees."

Neala's eyes flare with fire, but I watch as her pulse jumps in her neck, giving away how much she's enjoying the orders. She drops to her knees and waits as I unbuckle my leather belt and drop my zipper.

"Open your mouth." Her lips part on my order, and my cock throbs at the sight before me.

Gripping her hair, I guide her mouth to the tip of my cock. Neala snakes her tongue out and laps the droplet of pre-cum off my tip. I grind my teeth against the urge to fuck her mouth until I cum down her throat. When she wraps her plush lips around me, though, and swirls her hot tongue around the head, I'm gone.

I thrust my hips forward and pull her toward me. The head of my cock hits the back of her throat, and it constricts around me. I moan a cuss of pleasure. I look down to liquid honey eyes staring back at me, taking every inch I can fit in her mouth, and I spill hot spunk down her throat. Spurt after spurt, she swallows it all.

Completely spent, I pull my cock from her mouth and zip myself back in as Neala stands and delicately wipes the corner of her mouth.

"Mr Taylor," is all Neala says as she heads for the door to continue the day.

"Mistress."

I have a feeling this is the start of something either very good or very, very bad.

7

NEALA

Strutting from the office as calmly as I can without giving away just how much my heart is pounding against my ribs, I get myself away from Julian Taylor, my sub. *My sub!* What the . . . ?

All week I've tried to imagine Julian as my sub, wished for it even, but I just couldn't quite get a handle on it. The moment I saw that birthmark, I lost all sense of reality. I apparently also lost all sense and knowledge of being the Dom in this dynamic duo.

"On your knees." The deep command from Julian resounds around my head as I travel down floor after floor in the elevator. I shouldn't have done it, yet I'd wanted to. I'd wanted his cock deep in my throat and then I tasted him. And my God, he tastes so good!

The elevator slows and comes to a gradual halt, and the doors slide open. I step out, never once faltering as I walk through the main doors and to the car park. I pull open my car door and slink into the driver's seat. Not sure what I'm doing, or where I'm even going, I drive.

It isn't till I arrive at my apartment's parking that I realise what I've actually done: walked straight out without a word. I pull my phone from my handbag and begin to type a message.

I'm sorry I've . . . No, I hit the delete button.

We need to talk . . . Nope. I delete again.

Debating what I actually want, I begin to type again.

I suggest you arrive at my apartment within half an hour. You need putting back in your place. Mistress.

I hit the send button and watch as *delivered* pops up. A few moments later, it changes to *read*. Why should my heart still be pounding and my mouth feel as dry as Gandhi's flip-flop?

I'll be there in less than half an hour, Mistress. Sub.

Quickly I type in my address and I'm out of the car and heading for my apartment door before my pointless anxiety does anything else out of character.

My aching, heeled feet race me up and into my bathroom before I even realise it, an uneasy nervousness hot on my tail—a feeling I'm not used to having. *What is Julian doing to me?*

Closing the bathroom door behind me, I lean against it and place my hand firm against my racing heart. The flutter of butterflies dances behind my ribs, and the throbbing of my greedy cunt has my mind pouring over every hot and dirty deed I want to do to my new sub.

I can't wait to remind him of his place in our

relationship. *Relationship? Where the fuck did that thought come from?* Agreement. Yes, agreement is a much better term for what we have. A very mutually satisfying agreement.

With my thoughts utterly in the gutter, I turn my shower on, pull my hair into a high messy bun, and strip off all my clothes, pausing to stare at myself in the full-length mirror. My breasts feel heavy as I knead them roughly. I'm so ready for Julian right now.

Needing to hurry, I jump into the scorching hot stream of water. The heat of it burns deliciously over my skin as it covers me, and I particularly like the way it bites at my already aching nipples. With no patience to waste any more time, I quickly but thoroughly wash my body clean with a soft musk body wash, making sure to keep my head and hair out of the spray.

Just as I step out of the shower and turn off the water, my doorbell rings and I freeze to the spot. That was fast—did he sprint here or something?

I look at my towel laying across the rack, but before I reach for it an idea comes to mind that has me smiling wickedly. With confident movements, I stride out of the bathroom and straight to my front door, leaving wet footprints and drips in my wake along the hardwood floor. Thrusting my front door open, I find a wide-eyed and reddening Julian, his mouth agape, hair already dishevelled, and his pants instantly tenting as he looks me up and down.

His molten eyes land on mine and I snap hard, "Did I tell you that you can raise your eyes to mine?"

Without missing a beat, his gaze snaps to the floor and he lands heavily on his knees at my feet in the hallway of my apartment building, with me in the doorway, soaking wet and as naked as the day I was born. "I'm sorry, Mistress. I deserve to be punished."

Sorry, not sorry, Karen. I think of my nosey neighbour and smirk, wondering if she's getting an eyeful from her doorway. *But this is my time to play and I'm in charge here.*

JULIAN

The second I get the message from Mistress, I'm on my feet and running out the door, flying past the others working on my floor with a vague "Got to go" as I disappear into the elevator.

I don't think I've ever driven so fast in my life. The need to please Mistress rides me hard, and after taking control earlier, I feel uneasy inside. While it was sexy as hell, it isn't what I need. I'm always in charge in my family and work world, and letting myself go to be dominated is such an exhilarating and sexual thing for me.

"You need putting back in your place." I physically shiver as I remember her text. *Yes, please. Show me where I belong, Mistress. I need it.*

My foot pushes even harder on the accelerator, and my eyes keep flicking between the clock and the destination time on my satnav screen. I'm so close, yet so far.

Her apartment building comes into view, and I swerve my car into the guest parking out the front with perfect accuracy. *I'm coming, Mistress.* My hands push through my normally perfect hair, ruffling it with my frustration and need as I stride swiftly through the corridor and into the elevator.

I adjust myself in my pants as I step out at her floor, trying to keep some form of dignity while in public. *Stay calm dick, we're not there yet.* I give myself a mental talking to as I walk down the hallway toward her door number.

402. *Fuck, I'm here! Breathe.*

On a shaky inhale, I press my finger on her doorbell and listen impatiently to the light chiming coming from inside as my heart pounds against my chest.

My entire brain shuts down and malfunctions when a naked glistening body of perfection rips the door open —and I swear I stop breathing. The only part of my body still working is the rapidly hardening dick in my pants that only gets more painful as my gaze travels slowly up Mistress' body.

Her wet feet with the perfect French manicure, those smooth sensual legs that would feel heavenly wrapped around my head as I indulge myself in her perfect pussy. My eyes travel further still, knowing I shouldn't, but hey, I'm a glutton for punishment. I take in Neala's exquisite curvy frame topped with glorious tits, their pebbled nipples making my mouth water. My throat bobs as I swallow the need to kiss her plush bow-shaped lips, which were just phenomenal around my cock. Lastly, my eyes lock with hers. She pierces me with a fiery look of pure dominance, like the queen that she is, and my cock fucking jerks painfully, throbbing in my trousers.

"Did I tell you that you can raise your eyes to mine?" she demands, and my regret at disrespecting her authority is immediate. I drop to where I belong: at her feet.

Please don't turn me away. "I'm sorry, Mistress. I deserve to be punished."

Long delicate fingers grip at my hair and pull. I focus on not letting a moan of excitement leave me when she drags me into her apartment, making me shuffle along on my knees until she can shut the door behind us.

With one hand on the door handle, and the other still gripping my hair tightly, Mistress pulls me up and toward her wet heat as she opens her legs, putting one of them over my shoulder. "Eat it like it's gourmet," she demands. "But if you fail to satisfy me, you won't be allowed to taste my pussy again."

8

NEALA

Julian dives in like a man possessed. I know I said to eat it like it's gourmet, but damn, he's going at it like he's been lost in the desert for a week and my cunt is an endless supply of fresh water.

A low groan pours out of me, and my head falls back in pure ecstasy. The things this guy can do with his tongue should be illegal; it brings me so close to orgasm so fucking fast.

"Don't you fucking stop," I cry out, gripping his hair even harder. It must hurt like crazy, but instead of pulling back, Julian growls against me in pleasure at the bite of it and slides a finger I didn't ask for inside my dripping confines.

As much as I should punish him for acting without my command, I can't because the simple movement has my body shaking through a mind-blowing orgasm, and the only thing I can do is scream and clutch at the back of his head, probably smothering him to death.

My body starts jerking irregularly as his tongue continues the same assault, since I never gave him the order to cease. Instead of pushing him away, I force myself to ride it out and hold as still as I can. The torment I'm enduring is almost to the point of pain, but I know if I can get through it, a stronger and even more intense climax will be right around the corner.

It doesn't take long before I'm writhing against Julian's mouth again, and to his credit, he's still giving it his all, not letting tongue fatigue hinder his expertise in the slightest. His finger hasn't moved though, and now I desperately need it to, longing to feel it working me over like back in the office.

"Fuck me with your finger," I moan out in a low, husky voice, my legs now shaking as I use Julian's body and the door handle to keep me standing upright—but it's bloody hard.

I feel Julian smile against my pussy at my words as he starts to finger me in just the right way, and I make note of his smug movement for later. His skilled digit curls along my G-spot with every push, sending me dangerously close to spiralling.

My legs tremble even more, and Julian uses his other arm to help hold me up as I cry out, "Another finger."

Without delaying a second, a thicker finger enters me in time with the other one, and within four strokes, I'm done for. Julian holds me tight and close to stop me from dropping to the floor as my pussy squirts furiously all over his face, his mouth licking and slurping up as much as he can while he moans in appreciation.

I shakily say, "Stop," as I weakly push his head away.

Julian pulls his wet face back and helps me take my practically vibrating leg off his shoulder, then holds my legs together to steady them on the ground until I feel confident enough to walk again. *Note to self, don't try that again on only one leg.*

After I catch my breath and my heart rate calms a little bit, I look down at Julian, who's still on his knees. Luckily for him, he's looking down at the floor. "Good job, sub of mine. Keep that up and I might just keep you," I purr as I stroke his hair softly. "Unfortunately"—I yank his head back by his hair—"you're also in trouble. Tell me what you did?"

His eyes widen in a mixture of excitement and fear as he looks up at me. "I used my finger without your permission, Mistress," he admits straight away and without excuse.

"And?" I say softly, bringing my hand under his chin. Lifting his head higher, I bend myself over to come face to face with him. "What? You didn't think I'd notice you smiling at my need?" I *tsk,* shaking my head. "I can't be having that kind of defiance, now can I?"

"No, Mistress," Julian whispers, his eyes hooding with lust, and I look down at his lap to see a very hard cock crying out for my attention. And who am I to deny such an impressive thing?

Reaching down, I unzip Julian's pants, pleased he went commando today. Wrapping my hand around his sizeable girth, I garner an immediate hiss from him. I stroke up and down gently, using his own pre-cum to add an extra slide to it, before squeezing him tightly in my fist and pulling upward. "Follow me."

Julian instantly rises for me, his eyes lowered and his mouth closed like a good boy, and I turn and lead him to my bedroom with his dick. I let him go, telling him to use my en suite and return to me naked. Unhurried, I stroll across the room and open one of my drawers while he does as he's told, pulling out a pair of heavy-duty leather handcuffs before securing them to the bedhead, ready for use.

When he enters the room again, revealing himself in all his God-given glory, I guide him to the bed, telling him to lie down in the centre, and he listens to me without any hesitation. I almost feel bad for what I have planned for him. *Almost.* He needs to be taught a lesson in obedience one way or another, and I think this will be fun for the both of us.

As he lays waiting on his back in the middle of the bed, I climb up him, avoiding his twitching cock, and straddle his large body. "Lift your hands up, baby." It's not a term I'd usually use, but it feels right in the moment, and I always follow my gut.

Julian lifts his hands up to the straps I prepared earlier, and I wrap his wrists in the expensive leather, careful to have them tight but still comfortable. He has to work tomorrow, after all, and leaving bruised or red marks on him would be inconsiderate of me as his Mistress. I may be the dominant part of our relationship, but it's my duty of care to make sure Julian is well taken care of at all times.

Slowly I move down his body until my mouth lines up with his dick and I blow on it, watching in fascination as it twitches and bounces. Needing to taste Julian's salty flavour, I swirl the tip of my tongue around the head, before moving lower and taking in one of his balls and sucking deeply on it.

Julian draws in a sharp breath but squeezes his lips together to stop himself from making any unauthorised sounds. It pleases me to no end that he already seems to be working on his obedience, and I haven't even started the lesson yet.

"You can make whatever noise you want to. I give you permission to cry out," I tell him, wanting to hear his need, and my excitement builds at the idea of watching him fall apart.

Before he can answer me, I take his entire cock in my mouth and let it disappear down the back of my throat, the thickness threatening to choke me as it cuts off my airway, but I love it like that when it's on my terms.

His hips jerk off the bed involuntarily, and he cries out at the sudden movement, which pushes his cock even deeper inside my throat. I start to bob up and down, the sounds of Julian's desperation turning me on and spurring my movements to become more fervent.

I gag and saliva drips unchecked from my mouth as he bucks wildly at the pleasurable assault. *That's it, baby, take everything I'm giving you.*

Taking notice as his movements and breathing

slightly change, I know he's going to cum any second now. With one hard suck, I pop off the end and sit back before Julian can finish. I watch in satisfaction as his body trembles under me with need—his cock red and swollen, balls high and tight, and head leaking—craving release.

My eyes travel up his sexy abs and to his chiselled face, his gorgeous eyes locked onto me, pleading with words he knows he's not allowed to utter. *Please. More. Finish me. Make me cum. I need you.* All words he'll be punished for if he speaks them because we both know this is his discipline, not his treat.

I lift my leg over him and slide off the bed, going back to my drawer of tricks and pulling out my DP vibrator and clit sucker. One of us is going to have lots of happy endings today, and it's not Julian.

9

JULIAN

It took all my strength to keep my mouth shut and not cry out at the loss of Mistress' hot mouth wrapped around me, sucking me down like a hoover.

My eyes don't leave her sexy naked form as she glides across the room, opening up a drawer and producing two items that have me swallowing hard. By the looks of them, they're for her and not me, and I can't wait to see what she's going to do with them. I wonder if I can cum just from watching her . . .

Mistress approaches me with a wicked smile and lays beside me on the bed facing the opposite way. She opens her legs and places one smooth thigh over my midsection and the other as wide as she can, so I have a full view of her glistening pussy. *Fuck!*

The toys she's chosen are placed by her side before

she slides the fingers of her dominant hand between her soaking wet folds, rubbing her juices down to her asshole several times. Mistress' moans ring out as she fingers herself, pumping in and out of her pussy, eliciting sensual wet sounds that make me shudder with the need to be inside her. The middle finger on her hand lowers to her puckered hole and slowly pushes in and out, occasionally alternating between both holes to help lubricate her.

As both fingers thrust deep inside, Mistress' hips lift higher, giving me an epic unhindered view as her breathing turns to pants and her wetness increases to an unfathomable amount. My gaze fixates on every movement, and I couldn't look away if I tried. My cock pulses harder and more painful than ever, and my hips wiggle with the urge to be touched.

Mistress reaches beside her and picks up a double-dicked sex toy, licking and sucking on both ends to get them thoroughly saturated with spit. I watch, fascinated, as she lowers it between her legs, lining up both members with each hole and gently rolling her hips to glide them inside her, her breath hitching at the extra intrusion.

With slow, methodical movements, Mistress manages to fully seat her new accessory deep inside her, and I crave to suck on her little swollen nub, all left out. Mistress starts to fuck herself with it, at first slowly, but as she builds up her pleasure, the speed and pressure picks up. Before I know it, we're both panting hard. Her, with ecstasy, and me with pure lust at the sexiest show I've ever had the privilege of seeing.

Suddenly, Mistress reaches over for a smaller toy, which looks like a little plastic rose. She turns it on, and a discreet noise emanates from it as she lowers it to her clit, but the small device rips out a large response from her instantly. Her hips lift, and her thigh across my body begins to shake as one hand holds the rose still, while the other starts to pump her DP toys at a speedy, irregular pace, telling me she is dangerously close to cumming.

My dick pulses painfully, but I refuse to make any sound out of turn. I know my place, and I know what Mistress wants from me—I won't let her down again.

A scream rips through the air as Mistress pulls out her toy and flings her head back, lost to rapture, and it's fucking beautiful. Pussy juices soak my side and the bed in bursts as she rides her pleasure, the flower still connected but shaking from the force of her orgasm.

The climax is barely over before her curvaceous body straddles me once again, this time with her still-pulsing pussy swallowing my dick whole in one swift movement, both of our groans intermingling from the impalement.

Rolling her perfect hips, Mistress rides me hard and fast, right until my dick is ready to explode inside her. Just before I can reach the peak of my need, she lifts her body off mine and hops off the bed.

"You didn't really think it would be that easy, did you?" she seductively purrs from the doorway. "It's going to be a long night for you, baby. I'll get you some water to hydrate because you're going to need it."

Fuck. I wonder if this can kill me, I think to myself,

holding in a groan of protest as I look down at my aching cock.

"Would you like a snack too, baby?" Mistress asks, popping her head back around the doorframe with a wide smile that lights up her beautiful eyes. "I want to make sure you have everything you need while you're in my care. Well, not *everything*." She giggles at her own joke, and I smile back, feeling genuinely happy despite my punishment. Or maybe because of it?

At least I know Neala is the best kind of Mistress; she always watches for my body's queues for discomfort and keeps me well looked-after. Her tender care isn't missed by me, and I could very well grow to love her for that.

NEALA

With pure satisfaction, I finish off my make-up in the bathroom mirror, randomly sneaking a peek at the devastatingly handsome and frustrated man beside me as he shaves.

All through the night, I would wake and sexually torment Julian, making sure he never reached any kind of satisfaction—and not once did his obedience crumble. I'm not sure if I'm super proud of him or feel super bad for him.

Deciding that he has almost endured enough, I tell him as I fix his tie carefully, "Be a good boy for me today and I'll give you an extra special treat. All you have to do is not touch this until I say you can." I reach down and grab his crotch tight enough to feel good, and I watch as his eyes close and his tongue dips out to lick his lips.

"Yes, Mistress," he replies, his voice cracking with the strain of his unfulfilled desire.

With a wide smile, I stand up to my full height and say in a professional tone. "I'll see you in the office, Mr Taylor. You leave first, and I won't be far behind." I make it clear with my body language—turning to the side, away from him—that he is to leave immediately, and the scene is over.

I follow him to the front door, but before he steps through, I instruct, "Stay hydrated today and try to eat some protein. Breakfast might not have been enough."

Julian turns and smiles, his gaze always lower than my eyes. "I'll make sure to do that, Neala. Thank you for your concern."

With that, he strides off confidently down the hall, like an entirely different man.

The day goes smoothly after I arrive at work, and I get a small kick out of watching Julian randomly squirm in discomfort, especially when I let a little of my skin flash for him, such as when I went all 'Basic Instinct' on him earlier from across the room during a meeting. I knew foregoing my knickers would pay off.

As we walk toward the afternoon conference room for a company meeting, I pull Julian aside and ask quietly, "Have you been a good boy for me?"

His eyes light up like a kid on Christmas morning. "Yes, Mistress," he whispers back so nobody else can hear.

"Then you deserve a reward. I'm very proud of you." I softly stroke down his arm, making sure no one is watching, and as I walk in front of him, I make sure to slide my palm against his cock.

We enter the large room and I take a seat near the end of the table, using my eyes to motion for Julian to sit beside me. He lowers himself casually and pulls in his chair as the big boss starts the meeting, drivelling on about clients, costs, and other boring shit.

I inconspicuously slide my hand into Julian's lap and slowly pull his zip down while looking at the front as if they have my full attention. Julian stiffens under my touch—both his body in general, and the cock I spring free from its confines.

There is no way on earth he's going to last more than a minute after the way I kept him on edge all night and have been teasing him all day. With the amount of pre-cum I already feel, it tells me my instincts are right. I hope he knows how to stay quiet—or this is going to be a very interesting meeting.

Sliding my hand up and down his girth, I make a point not to look at him and not move my arm above the elbow. I listen gleefully at his increase in quiet breathing beside me; he's doing an excellent job keeping himself under control, but I can notice it because I'm looking for it.

Julian's hips start to lift, and I casually lean over and

grab a tissue from the box that's always on the table, careful not to stop my one-handed ministrations. I pretend to wipe my nose and then pass it to him under the table, knowing he's about to blow. He quickly takes it from me and barely makes it on time as he jerks slightly, some of his warm seed spilling onto my hand.

Using a small cough to cover his response, he leans forward to grab another tissue with his spare hand, while trying to clean up his mess without raising any suspicion in the room. Luckily, the boss and one of the senior lawyers are having a heated discussion, garnering everyone else's attention.

I manage to suppress my satisfied smirk as I hear the soft telltale sign of his zipper and am glad no one has the mind to pay any attention to what's going on over here.

"What are your thoughts, Taylor?" They all turn to a slightly pink-cheeked Julian, seeking an answer, and I hope he was listening because I have no idea what they were talking about.

Julian fidgets in his chair slightly but gives a beaming smile down the table. "Honestly, I am on Dell's side this time. A charity event of a high enough calibre could really bring up morale after the company's price hike, and you know a lot of our clients love any excuse to get all dressed up and throw their money around. They have the money to match our fees, after all, but giving them a reason to show it off in front of their rivals is a sure-fire way to keep them loyal."

The room laughs heartily, and they all start bouncing

ideas around about what kind of charity will benefit from the wealthy clientele's money.

I smile and nod approvingly at Julian, and his eyes beam with pride at my acknowledgement. In that moment, I know he's the right fit for me, and I seem to be the right fit for him.

Time to go shopping.

10

FOUR WEEKS LATER

JULIAN

It feels like a lifetime ago since I first came to Neala's apartment, and now I'm here a few times a week, when summoned of course. I'd never turn up here without being asked—I don't think I'd like to go through the punishment of pleasure without release again. Though I also fucking loved it at the same time.

My cock jerks in my trousers at the thought of the hand job Neala gave me in the conference room the day after. Thinking of the Devil, in glides the being of my every fantasy.

"Mr Taylor." Neala's voice holds a note of authority, and my cock involuntarily jerks again.

We've already had some fun this morning, and now I'm ready to leave for work, ahead of Neala as always.

I address Neala as I should. "Mistress?"

A hint of a smile plays at the corners of her sensual lips. "Tonight, when we finish at the office, I want you to go home and get ready for a trip to Dom X."

Tamping down the excitement the club's name fires through me, I agree and wait for permission to leave, which comes shortly after. I head for the front door, but just as my hand is about to connect with the cool metal of the handle, Neala's voice sounds again, close behind me and just a whisper.

"And, sub, make sure you're ready for what's going to happen tonight. I want to see how far you'll really go for me."

"Yes, Mistress." My voice hitches, no longer hiding the excitement of anticipation. I clear my throat and try again. "Yes, Mistress."

Then I head out the door, heart bouncing off my ribs, knowing I've got to spend all day wondering what's in store for me later.

We arrive at the parking lot for Dom X, and I'm still a little baffled that Neala told me we could travel together tonight, as I always meet her here. She hasn't spoken to me the last five minutes of the drive, and I can't help but think she's feeling nervous for some reason, which shouldn't give me the male satisfaction I'm feeling, but it does. Defiance still lives in me; even though I like to be dominated by Neala, it doesn't mean I'm not still masculine to the core.

As we get to the bar, Neala greets her friend Jasmine and hands her a small box, but I think little of it. Most likely, it's a cock ring for Jasmine's sub, like they were discussing a week ago.

I fidget with the mask on my face, trying to make it sit right so I can see.

"Sub, are you ready?" Neala's voice snaps me to attention.

"Yes, Mistress." I wait for her to lead me to one of the back rooms, but to my slight shock, she leads me to the stage. I don't falter in my step, though. Neala is what and who I've been looking for since I accepted this is who I am.

I follow her up the three steps, and the buzz going on in the club begins to dull to chatter as people realise what's going on. Every fibre in me is alive with what's about to happen—and now I know why Neala was feeling nervous. This right here is her showing everyone I'm hers and hers alone. She's staking her claim, or in other words, declaring a relationship between us. Hell of a way to announce it, too.

The room falls silent as we get to centre stage. Neala turns around and I drop to my knees, head bowed. Waiting.

"You're mine, sub." Neala's voice rings with dominance and a shiver skitters its way over my body.

"And to prove it, I'm going to fuck you in front of everyone here."

Cheers and whoops sound out around the room, and I suppress the smile threatening to spread across my face.

"Strip." The command comes, and I'm undressing before I know it, so used to obeying now.

I don't even register those watching; I'm focused on Neala, and her alone. Not that I mind being watched—it's just more of a turn on.

NEALA

Watching Julian drop to his knees has all kinds of feelings running through me, most of which head directly between my legs.

"Strip." I demand. I want and need to see those toned, rippling muscles that cover every inch of this man before me. This man that my 'feelings' have grown for—more than I could imagine they would for anyone. Destined to be alone forever, I thought. Well, apparently not. From the moment he walked into the office, I'd thought about him on his knees for me. That moment I saw his birthmark sealed the deal on—hopefully—the rest of my life.

Looking down at a now naked Julian makes my mouth water and my pussy slick. Yeah, I've made a hell of a good choice here.

I pull the whip from my knee–length boot, having tucked it in there earlier. I run the leather whip up Julian's honed torso, coming to rest under his chin. I tip his head back and his eyes lock with mine, swimming with desire as they do.

"First thing you're going to do while everyone watches"—I raise a brow, impressed that he doesn't even seem bothered about our audience; in fact, I think he's enjoying it—"is you're going to eat my pussy and then my ass." His eyes become even heavier with desire at that. "Now watch me as I strip."

Julian's intense gaze never leaves my body as I strip naked. His eyes run a scorching path over every inch of skin I reveal to him—to everyone. Once fully naked, I take my position on the stage. Learning from my mistake of standing up, I sit and lean back on my elbows. Then I let my legs fall away from each other, exposing my slick, dripping cunt to Julian. Who waits patiently for my command. But he doesn't stop himself from biting his lower lip, and the rise and fall of his chest becomes rapid, almost feral. His impressive cock visibly throbs as pearls of pre-cum glisten on the head.

"You hungry?" I taunt.

"Yes, Mistress." Julian's voice is deep and holds an edge of that feralness.

"Then feast."

The words aren't even finished leaving my mouth when Julian's mouth locks over my pussy. His tongue swirls and flicks and my hips buck under his erotic assault. Closer and closer, he pushes me to the edge. He's learnt every button to press on me to make me cum, and I can't help but love every second. With one last flick of his tongue, my release barrels into me.

"Stop."

Julian rocks back on his heels, panting, mouth wet from my juices. I roll onto my knees, spreading my legs, and drop my tits to the hard, cold wood of the stage. My nipples pebble against the bite of the coolness, and the sensation zaps through my body.

I wiggle my hips and the flat of Julian's tongue connects with my ass, and just like my pussy, he feasts like a glutton. I moan as he pushes his tongue into my ass.

"Fingers," I whine out.

Two fingers spear knuckles deep into my pussy, lubing them up before tracking to my tight asshole. Removing his tongue, he eases one in.

"More!" I demand.

The second plunges in alongside the first. I begin to push back as he fucks my ass with his fingers, but I want more.

On cue, a bottle of lube is thrown onto the stage, along with a strap-on, *my* strap-on. Slamming back into reality, I remember it's me who should be fucking Julian's ass, but in all honesty, I'm too far gone.

"In my ass, now, sub!" The need in my voice has Julian lubing his dick up in double time. We have both supplied each other with clean health checks so we can safely do this without protection, and I have an IUD to prevent any other 'issues.'

The head of his cock pushes in and the exquisite sting of pain has me pushing back, taking more inches. Needing no more prompting, Julian slams in deep and hard, and I cry out.

In and out, deeper and harder. I take a peek at the onlookers, and those with subs are joining in with their own fun, pussies being eaten, cocks being sucked, asses spanked. Spectacular sight. But nothing like the cock slamming into me.

I want his cum in my pussy though. I pull off his cock, and Julian grabs my hips to pull me back.

Bad. Move.

Before he can disobey again, I grab the strap-on and get to my feet, legs shaking.

"Bend over." Slight anger fills my voice and without hesitation, Julian spins and bends over.

I pull the strap-on up and secure it in place. Rubbing lube up and down the length of the silicone cock, I position myself behind him. "I'm not going to go easy on you. Grabbing me when I moved away?" I push the head of the strap-on in, and I watch his ass muscles flex, taking the pain. "What did you think you were doing?" I push further in, knowing he won't answer because my questions are rhetorical. "I told you not to disobey again, didn't I?"

I thrust the length deep into his ass and hear the pleasurable pain leave him on a shuddered moan.

And then I pound.

Harder and deeper. Gripping his left hip, I spank his ass with my right hand, watching his cheek turn pink, knowing it's causing some pain because my palm stings with each strike. I see my whip just in reach and grasp it in my hand, instantly bringing it down on his ass, knowing he relishes the pain.

I don't falter in my rhythm. Even though my legs are burning, I ignore it. No pain, no gain, right?

Julian's body begins to shake, signalling I'm pushing him closer to spilling hot spunk everywhere.

I'm ready to let it happen. "Cum for me, Julian." With one last deep thrust, his body arches forward and he orgasms so hard his ass kicks back at me, pushing on the strap-on and prolonging his orgasm.

Completely spent, Julian just flops down and lies on his front, panting hard, sweat glistening his muscled back with each inhale and exhale.

I stand and remove the strap-on, then dress myself. I go to Julian and begin to help him into his clothes while he recovers. When he's dressed, I grab his hair in front of our audience, who have also all finished, and I kiss him deep. Cheers and claps resound, and I smile against his lips, feeling him do the same.

"Come on, to the bar," I say, rising to my feet again.

"You called me Julian, not sub." It's nothing more than a statement, and I let it slide, considering it was my hiccup, not his.

When we get to the bar, I point for Julian to sit at my feet next to Jasmine's pet, and he does so obediently. With a smile at my friend, I reach over and take the box back from her and she does the movie screen slow clap.

"Now that's what I call a hot performance. He's going to feel that punishment every time he sits down for the next few days." She laughs softly and strokes her pet's hair.

I gingerly open the box before me and pluck out my

specially made long, leather, braided band with a simple platinum ring on the end. Long enough to hide under Julian's everyday work clothes, but still short enough to make my point.

Leaning down, I pull Julian's chin up so he's looking me in the eye. It's not something I would usually allow, but I want him to understand the significance of my actions and also the weight of the feelings I've developed for him.

"You have earned my trust, my loyalty, and my love," I start, as I wrap my arms around his neck and do up the back of the necklace I'm gifting him. "This is to signify my ownership of you. All of you. I expect you to never share your body, your submission, or your heart with anyone but me from now on. Understand?"

Even though I sound in charge, it's well known in this community that it's actually the subs who have all the power. Without their trust in us, and their consent, we would have nothing. The vulnerability of what I'm asking for is unfamiliar to me, but if he accepts what I have to offer, then it's all worth it.

Julian's eyes widen for a fraction of a second before warming, and his simple words tell me everything I need to know, setting my nerves to rest.

"Yes, Mistress."

SOCIAL MEDIA

Soul Sisters
Linktree:
https://linktr.ee/soul.sisters.novels

Alexandra K. Martin
Linktree:
https://linktr.ee/alexandrakmartin

BOOKS BY SOUL SISTERS

-Dom X (MF Erotic)

-Releasing the Beast (MF PNR Horror Romance-Coming 2024)